For my parents and brother, thanks for all your support. – TM

For Beck. And for Dad, Mum and Hannah. Thank you for everything. – MS

The ABC 'Wave' device and the 'ABC KIDS' device are
trademarks of the Australian Broadcasting Corporation and are
used under licence by HarperCollins*Publishers* Australia.

First published in Australia in 2012
by HarperCollins*Children's Books*
a division of HarperCollins*Publishers* Australia Pty Limited
ABN 36 009 913 517
harpercollins.com.au

HarperCollins*Publishers*
Level 13, 201 Elizabeth Street, Sydney, NSW 2000, Australia
Unit D1, 63 Apollo Drive, Rosedale, Auckland 0632, New Zealand
A 53, Sector 57, Noida, UP, India
1 London Bridge Street, London SE1 9GF, United Kingdom
2 Bloor Street East, 20th floor, Toronto, Ontario M4W 1A8, Canada
195 Broadway, New York NY 10007, USA

National Library of Australia Cataloguing-in-Publication entry:

Miller, Tim.
There is a monster under my bed who farts / Tim Miller; illustrated by Matt Stanton.
ISBN: 978 0 7333 3125 1 (hbk.)
For children.
Flatulence–Juvenile fiction.
Monsters–Juvenile fiction.
Stanton, Matt.
Australian Broadcasting Corporation.
A823.4

Designed and typeset by Matt Stanton
The illustrations in this book were hand-drawn and digitally coloured
Colour reproduction by Graphic Print Group, Adelaide
Printed in China by RR Donnelley on 128gsm Matt Art

14 13 12 11   15 16 17 18

THERE IS A MONSTER UNDER MY BED WHO FARTS

TIM MILLER + MATT STANTON

ABC Books

There is a **monster**
under my **bed** who **farts.**

You **never** want to use the bathroom after him.

His **belly** grumbles so loudly
I can't hear my **cartoons.**

And he's **silent** and **deadly**
in a small space.

There is a **monster** in our supermarket who farts.

You **don't** want to pull **his** finger.

His **balloons** are filled with more than just hot air.

And he **loves** to blow out the candles

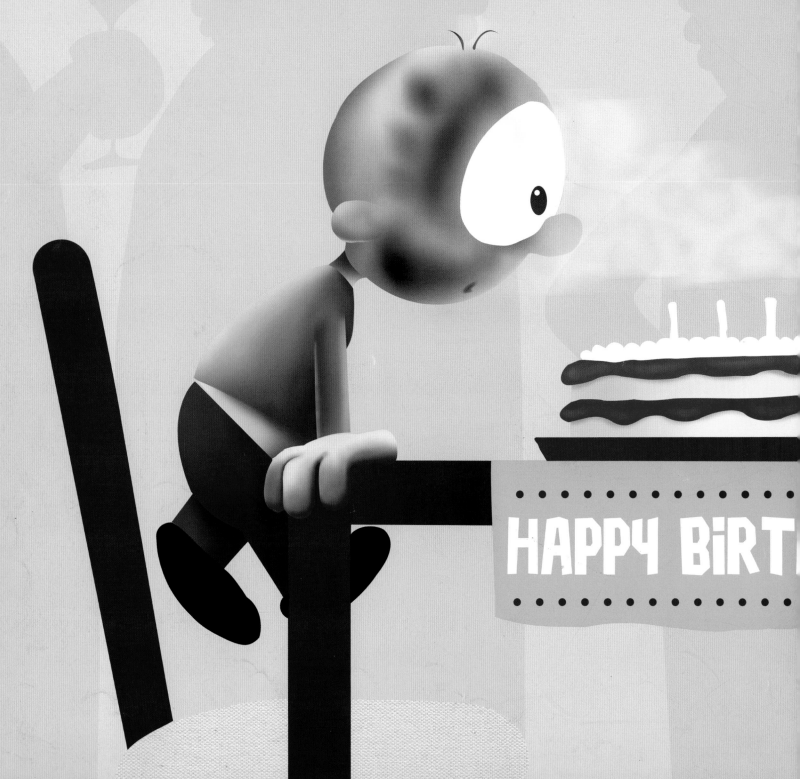

(even when it's not his birthday).

'It wasn't me!'

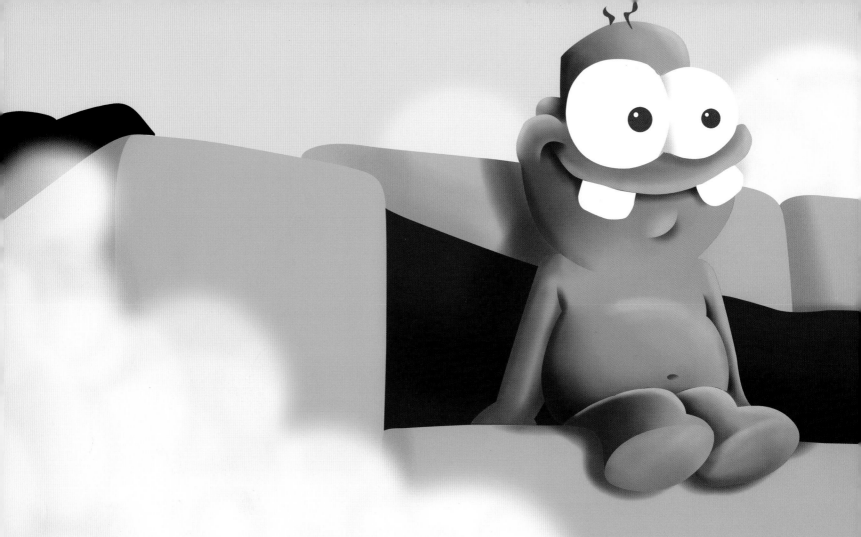

There is a **monster**
on the **couch** who **farts**.

He's trying to compete with **Dad!**

There is a **monster**
under our bench who **farts**.

Mum thinks there's a gas leak!

There is a monster
in my bath who farts ...

I WISH

'There is a monster
in my bed who farts!'

Why don't they believe me?